Sasha and the Bicycle Thieves

Errol Lloyd

Michael

Tunde

Kelly

Sasha

Tava

Nadine

Illustrated by
THE AUTHOR

New York • Toronto

First edition for the United States and Canada published 1989
by Barron's Educational Series, Inc.

First published 1988 by William Heinemann Ltd.,
Michelin House, 81 Fulham Road, London SW3 6RB

All inquiries should be addressed to:
Barron's Educational Series, Inc.
250 Wireless Boulevard
Hauppauge, NY 11788

International Standard Book No. 0-8120-6141-1

Library of Congress Catalog Card No. 89-421

Library of Congress Cataloging-in-Publication Data

Lloyd, Errol.
    Sasha and the Bicycle Thieves/Errol Lloyd; illustrated by
the author—1st ed. for the U.S. and Canada.
        p.   cm.—(Banana book)
    Summary: When her new BMX bike is stolen, Sasha enlists
the help of her friends in tracking down a ring of bicycle
thieves.
    ISBN 0-8120-6141-1
    [1. Crime and criminals—Fiction. 2. Bicycles and
bicycling—Fiction.] 1.Title II. Series: Banana book series.
PZ7.L776Sas   1989
[E]—dc19   89-421
                                CIP
                                AC

PRINTED IN HONG KONG

901   9903   987654321

Chapter 1

SASHA PRESSED THE brakes on her
brand new BMX bicycle and brought it
to a screeching halt—just in time to
avoid crashing into a large green and
yellow limousine that shot out from a
side street.

"Why don't you look where I am
going!" shouted the uniformed
chauffeur behind the steering wheel.

"You little maniac!" scowled a man in a yellow suit from the back seat, his fat face hidden behind a large pair of dark glasses. "You could have scratched my newly resprayed, air-conditioned, fully automatic Silver Cloud 1 Rolls-Royce."

"With power steering and chauffeur-

driven," chipped in the chauffeur.

"That's not fair," shouted Sasha. "It wasn't my fault." But before Sasha could get the words out of her mouth, the green and yellow Rolls-Royce sped off down the road, leaving a cloud of dust behind it.

Sasha was very upset and decided to push the bicycle the rest of the way to the basement headquarters of the BRAT Club (BRAT stands for Bicycle Riders Action Team). She had her application form with her and today was going to be her big day. She had to take a riding test as well as a road safety test. If she passed both tests she would become a full member of BRAT.

Sasha was sure she would succeed. She was already a good rider, but that wasn't enough to get her into the BRAT Club. She had to be able to do much more and she had spent a lot of time practicing on her new bike.

First, she had to be able to bring the bicycle to a quick and safe stop. She knew from what had just happened with the green and yellow Rolls-Royce that she was bound to pass that part of the test. In addition, she had to be able to ride in a straight line drawn in chalk on the sidewalk, and to ride in a tight circle, turning both to the left and to the right, without wobbling. Finally, she had to be able to control the bike by riding with only one hand on the handlebar while signaling with the other hand.

Even if she did all these things correctly, she still had to be able to give the right answers to questions on the Bicycle Safety Test, like how to cross the road with her bike and how to pass parked vehicles. She also had to know the meaning of road signs and how to take care of her bike and keep it in good working order.

But right now Sasha was still shaking with a mixture of anger and fright from her terrifying experience with the Rolls-Royce. She had completely forgotten about the test as she leaned her bike against the fence and scampered down the steps to the basement door, which had the words BRAT CLUB—STRICTLY PRIVATE written on it.

She knocked three times and called out the secret password. The door opened.

Chapter 2

SASHA ENTERED THE room and was
met by the five members of the BRAT
Club.

Tunde, who had started the Club with
his sister, Nadine, was busy making new
membership cards. "You look as if
you've just seen a ghost," he said.

"This enormous car nearly knocked

me over," said Sasha. "But it wasn't my fault," she added quickly. She didn't want them to think that she had been careless, especially on the day she was going to take her riding test.

"Are you OK?" asked Tara who was one of her best friends.

"I'm fine," said Sasha. "But I hope I don't meet those mean men in that car again."

Kelly and Michael, who had been leafing through the pages of a cycling magazine, joined the little group which had gathered around Sasha as she related the events of the two horrible men in the green and yellow Rolls-Royce.

"Do you still want to take your test?" asked Tunde.

"Of course I do," said Sasha, who was determined to become a member of the BRAT Club as soon as possible.

Kelly, who had passed his test only the week before, went over to the table and picked up a test sheet and a pen to write down the results of each test.

"Alright now," he said. "Where's your bike?"

"It's outside," said Sasha, who only then realized that she had broken one of the first rules of the BRAT Club, which was to keep your bike in a safe place at all times. They followed Sasha up the steps as she hurriedly made her way to her bike.

"It's gone," said Sasha. "My bike is gone. I left it right there," she exclaimed, pointing to the empty spot near the fence. "Someone must have stolen it."

Almost in tears, she looked around for any sign of her bike. In the distance she could see a fat man in a yellow suit pushing a bicycle.

"It's him!" exclaimed Sasha. "It's one of the men in the car that nearly knocked me over. Stop! Thief! That's my bike. Bring it back," she shouted down the road after him.

The fat man started to run, but the gang chased after him. He mounted the bike and wobbled along for a few feet before picking up speed.

"Bring back my bike!" screamed Sasha, but the thief was now pedaling fast into the distance.

He turned the corner and it was a few seconds before Sasha and the others caught up. They were just in time to see him shove Sasha's bike into the trunk of the green and yellow Rolls-Royce, before hopping into the back seat. Then with a screeching of tires and a puff of smoke, the Rolls-Royce raced down the road.

"Quick," said Sasha to Kelly, "write down the license plate number of the car. It's 628 BUG."

"We'd better go to the police right away," said Tunde.

Chapter 3

"Now let me get this straight," said the police officer, looking at Sasha and the members of the BRAT Club in disbelief. "First you nearly get run over by a chauffeur-driven Rolls-Royce, then later the same two men in the same car steal your bicycle and drive off with it . . ?"

"Don't forget the dark glasses and the yellow suit," chipped in another officer, who was seated at the other end of the counter.

"Of course not," said the first officer. "And we must note that the driver was dressed up in a chauffeur's uniform."

"But it's true," said Sasha. "We've even got the license plate number of the car to prove it."

With this, Kelly triumphantly produced the slip of paper with the number 628 BUG written on it.

The officer took the slip of paper and examined it. "Check this out will you, Joe," he said to the seated officer. He tapped his fingers on the counter and waited, while his colleague fed the information into the computer with a few taps of his finger on the keyboard.

Within moments, Joe handed him a sheet of paper from the computer.

"Now let's see what the computer

printout has to say," he said. "Car license number 628 BUG belongs to a white Chevy which was involved in an accident ten years ago and sold for scrap. The last owner was a Miss Priscilla Brown."

"It's not April Fool's day, is it Joe?" With a twinkle in his eye, the policeman wrote down all the details on a pad. Sasha's name and address, the color and make of her bike, where it was lost and a description of the thieves and the car they were driving.

"We'll keep a lookout for a fat man in a yellow suit with dark glasses riding a kid's red BMX," he said. "We've had a lot of reports of missing bicycles lately."

"It's no use," said Sasha to her friends as they left the police station. "They will never believe us."

Chapter 4

SASHA AND THE gang were dejected as
they made their way back to the BRAT
headquarters.

"I'm sure we got the number right,"
said Sasha.

"628 BUG," said Kelly, slowly
reciting the license plate number as if
it was there in front of him.

Tears welled up in Sasha's eyes as the

full tragedy of what had happened slowly sank in. "What am I going to say to my mom?" she sobbed. "How can I tell her I've lost the bike she bought me for my birthday? I've had it for only two weeks." With this, more tears came flooding down Sasha's cheeks.

"Never mind," said Tara, "We'll all help you to find your bike."

"Let's get some ice cream," said Nadine, who could always be relied upon to come up with bright ideas at the right time. At this, Sasha cheered up and they went into the candy store,

chipped in, and bought ice cream
for everybody.

For a time Sasha forgot her
troubles as they walked down the street
eating their ice cream. Suddenly a large
green and yellow car came into view. It
was being driven by a chauffeur in a
blue uniform and in the back seat sat a fat
man in a yellow suit and wearing a pair
of dark glasses.

"It's them," shouted Michael. "It's the
bicycle thieves."

"And look," said Kelly. "Look . . . the
license plate. It's 628 BUG." Without

stopping to think what they would do if they caught up with the thieves, the gang gave chase. It was the middle of the rush hour, and the traffic was not moving very fast, but somehow, each time they got close to the car, the traffic would start to move again.

Nadine had an idea. "Let's take a short-cut through the park," she said. "Then we can get to the corner before they do."

Keeping their eyes on the Rolls-Royce as it wormed its way through the traffic, they ran across the park. And

just as Nadine had thought, they got to
the corner before the car did.

"Here it comes," said Nadine excitedly.
But they all felt a little silly standing on
the corner, for there was no way that
they could get the car to stop. So how
could they get Sasha's bike back?

Then, quite unexpectedly, the car
turned off the main road and
disappeared down a side street. They
ran to the intersection and quickly
made their way down the side street.
They were just in time to see the Rolls-

Royce turn into an enormous gate
with stone lions seated on the pillars
that supported the gates. As the car
disappeared up the drive, the gates
automatically clanged shut behind it.

Sasha and the gang dashed over and
stood breathless in front of the gates,
their hearts beating with excitement
from the long chase.

"We'd better go to the police again,"
said Kelly. "They're bound to believe us
now."

"Fat chance," said Tunde. "They didn't
believe us when we said the thieves

were driving a Rolls-Royce. Why should they believe us when we tell them they live in a fancy mansion?"

"But what are we going to do?" asked Kelly. "We can't just let them get away with stealing Sasha's bike."

"We can't just stand here talking about it," said Michael. "We have to do something."

"I know what," said Sasha, with a touch of excitement in her voice. "We'll just have to do our own investigating."

Chapter 5

THE FIRST PROBLEM the gang faced was how to get beyond the massive iron gates in front of them. Tunde was the tallest, and with the help of Sasha and Michael, he clambered over the top and dropped lightly onto the grass on the other side. He made a dash for the control box that stood some five feet from the entrance. There he pressed a button marked "open" and watched the heavy gates slowly swing around.

The gang felt some safety in numbers as they crept toward a huge oak tree that stood halfway up the driveway. They bunched together behind the tree, considering what to do next.

"The car's bound to be there," said

Sasha, pointing to the garage at the side
of the house. "Let's get my bike and go."

Cautiously, the gang tiptoed toward
the house and hid behind some bushes
at the side of the garage. It was Tara's
turn to be daring and she quickly darted
to the garage and tried the door.

"It's not locked," she whispered, as the
door swung open to reveal the gleaming
green and yellow Rolls-Royce.

Trembling with excitement, Sasha opened the trunk of the car, but there was no sign of her bike.

"It's got to be around somewhere," said Tara. And that was when they noticed the door at the back of the garage.

Michael slowly opened it and they inched their way into the darkness, fumbling with their hands along the side of the wall in search of a light switch. It was Kelly who eventually found the switch and turned on the light.

What they saw took their breath away. For here was another garage, twice as big as the one with the Rolls-Royce, filled with row after row of bicycles. There must have been hundreds of them. There were bicycles of every make and description. There

were Raleighs, Choppers, BMX's, Yamahas, and more. But it didn't take Sasha long to spot her red BMX.

"There it is," she whispered. "Let's take it and get going."

But just as Sasha was about to wheel her bicycle away, they heard voices coming from outside the window at the side of the garage.

"Shhhhhh . . ." Sasha warned the others, as they silently crept over to the window. One by one, five heads peeped over the windowsill to see who was there. They were not in the least bit surprised to discover that the voices belonged to the two bicycle thieves.

Chapter 6

THE BICYCLE THIEVES were seated at
a patio table beside a heart-shaped
pool, sipping iced tea and munching
chocolate cookies.

"Brilliant operation," they heard the
fat man saying to the chauffeur.
Absolutely brilliant."

"Yeah, you was smart, Boss," echoed the chauffeur. "And you showed them kids that chased you how to ride a bike, didn't you, Boss?"

"Terrific stuff," said the fat man, stuffing two chocolate cookies into his mouth.

"Ten bikes in one day," said the chauffeur, rubbing his hands together gleefully. "How much do you think they'll bring us?"

"Well, they are all in good condition," said the fat man. "And that red one is as good as new. I guess we're talking about at least a thousand dollars at today's prices."

"Not a bad day's work," said the chauffeur, as he refilled their glasses with iced tea. "I guess in a year or two we'll be able to retire from this racket."

"Retire!" said the fat man. "Retire

from such an easy job? You must be joking. It's one of my most brilliant ideas," he continued. "Just pick up bikes off the street, clean 'em up, smuggle them out of the country and sell them for a hundred bucks each. A nice little income."

With that the two men roared with laughter.

"Mind you," he added, "It's getting a little risky when kids begin to chase you. Imagine trying to catch up with a fully automatic Rolls-Royce."

"With power steering and chauffeur-driven!" added the chauffeur.

"The best car in the world," said the fat man. And with that the two men laughed even louder than before.

Then the fat man turned in the direction of the garage. Sasha and the gang ducked their heads as quickly as they could.

"You left that darned light on again," the fat man howled at the chauffeur. "How many times have I told you not to leave that light on?"

"I didn't leave it on. I swear I didn't, Boss!"

"And the garage door. Did you lock it?"

"I was planning to lock it later."

"Later!" shrieked the fat man. "Well I think there's something fishy going on down there. I bet it's them kids . . . Let's go and take a look."

Sasha grabbed her bike and the other members of the BRAT Club took the first bikes they could lay their hands on. "Quick, let's get out of here," said Sasha.

Chapter 7

Sasha and the Bicycle Riders Action
Team pedaled their bikes furiously
toward the open gates at the end of
the driveway.

"Come back here, you blasted little
thieves," shouted the fat man. But there
was no stopping the gang now.

"After them," he instructed the

chauffeur as he hopped into the back of
the Rolls-Royce.

From a distance, the gang heard the
roar of the mighty Rolls-Royce engine
as the car backed out of the garage,
turned around in one smooth action, and
raced toward the little cluster of bikes
now approaching the gates.

"Don't forget the Bicycle Safety Test,"
shouted Tunde over his shoulder to the
others as they reached the intersection.
They crossed the road safely and
headed for the park.

As they cut across the park they could see the green and yellow outline of the Rolls-Royce, skirting the park in an attempt to get to the corner before they did.

"Follow me," said Tunde, who had quickly made up a plan of action.

Sasha did her best to keep up with the members of the Bicycle Riders Action Team, and pumped her bicycle pedals as fast as she could. They could see the Rolls-Royce bearing down on them, but by a stroke of luck, the traffic lights near the park gates turned red, just in time to force the Rolls-Royce to a violent halt.

"Hurry, hurry," said Tunde as they rode through the gates. Six hands signaled to the right as they swung out onto the street ahead of the Rolls-Royce.

It wasn't until they had passed the familiar candy store and rounded the corner that Tunde's plan became clear. For in the distance they would see the police station they had left only a short while before. Sasha and the gang never dreamed they would have been so glad to see the police station again so soon as they raced the last few feet to its open gates, beads of perspiration running down their faces.

The Rolls-Royce was still in hot pursuit as they glided their bikes across the entrance of the police station. Without realizing what he was doing, the chauffeur swung the Rolls-Royce through the gates, and got the fright of his life when he saw all the police vehicles parked there.

"It's a trap, you darned fool," shouted the fat man. "Turn around and get moving before we're caught."

But it was too late. A policeman had spotted the thieves chasing the gang and had radioed the station. The exit from the station was now blocked by a police van and patrol car, their lights flashing and sirens blasting.

The bicycle thieves were trapped. They came out of the Rolls-Royce with their hands held high in the air.

"Hurray," shouted Sasha and the gang at the tops of their voices.

Chapter 8

"628 BUG," wrote the policeman in his notebook, his face flushed with embarrassment, for it was the same officer who hadn't believed the gang when they reported the theft of Sasha's bike. "That's a false license plate number of course," he added sheepishly. "It really did belong to that white Chevy, but the thieves must have gotten the plate from a junkyard and put it on the Rolls."

"But why would they go to all that trouble?" inquired Sasha.

"Because the Rolls-Royce was also stolen," explained the officer. "They got rid of the real license plate and put this false one on so that the police couldn't trace it. They were clever enough to change the color as well," he added.

"Well done, kids," interrupted the captain as he entered the room with a tray laden with orange juice and cookies.

"We've recovered over two hundred bikes, all stolen from children. We'll have to put them on display and have an open day when the children can come and identify their bikes."

"But you must promise to leave such dangerous work to the police in the future," he said.

"We promise," said Sasha. "But will

you believe us next time?"

"Of course we will," laughed the captain, and with that they finished their snack. A reporter from the local newspaper came and Sasha and the gang told her the entire story, which she wrote down in shorthand on a pad.

As soon as they left the police station, Sasha took her riding test. She rode a faultless round and answered all the questions on the Bicycle Safety Test correctly.

"You're now a full member of the BRAT Club," said Nadine as she handed Sasha her membership card, with her name printed at the top in bold letters.

When Sasha returned home, she wheeled her bike into the hallway, took a dustrag and began to clean it.

"How did the test go?" asked her mom.

"I passed," said Sasha, flashing her membership card. "But at first I thought I wasn't going to be able to take my test. Two horrible men stole my bike but me and Tunde and Tara and the rest of the kids followed them into this big house and we found hundreds of stolen bikes in the garage. We rode off to the police station and the men chased us in their green and yellow Rolls-Royce . . ."

"Hold on, young lady," said Sasha's mom. "Sounds as if this should be dramatized for television!"

"You'll believe me when you read about it in the paper tomorrow," said Sasha. "It might even be on television, too," she added.

"You look tired and hungry," said her mom. "Have your dinner and get ready for bed."

Before Sasha went to bed she wheeled her bike into the shed in the backyard where she usually kept it. But this time she did something she had never done before. She took out her bicycle lock and chained her bike to the side of the shed.

"Just in case," she said.